P9-ELV-711

For my two big brothers, Emmanuel and Vincent

Thanks to Michel Lagarde

Kane/Miller Book Publishers, Inc.
First American Edition 2008
by Kane/Miller Book Publishers, Inc.
La Jolla, California

Originally published in France by Éditions du Rouergue under the title, "Juke-box" in 2007

Copyright © Éditions du Rouergue, 2007

Library of Congress Control Number:
Printed and bound in China
1 2 3 4 5 6 7 8 9 10

ISBN: 978-1-933605-72-2

Jukebox

Kane/Miller
BOOK PUBLISHERS

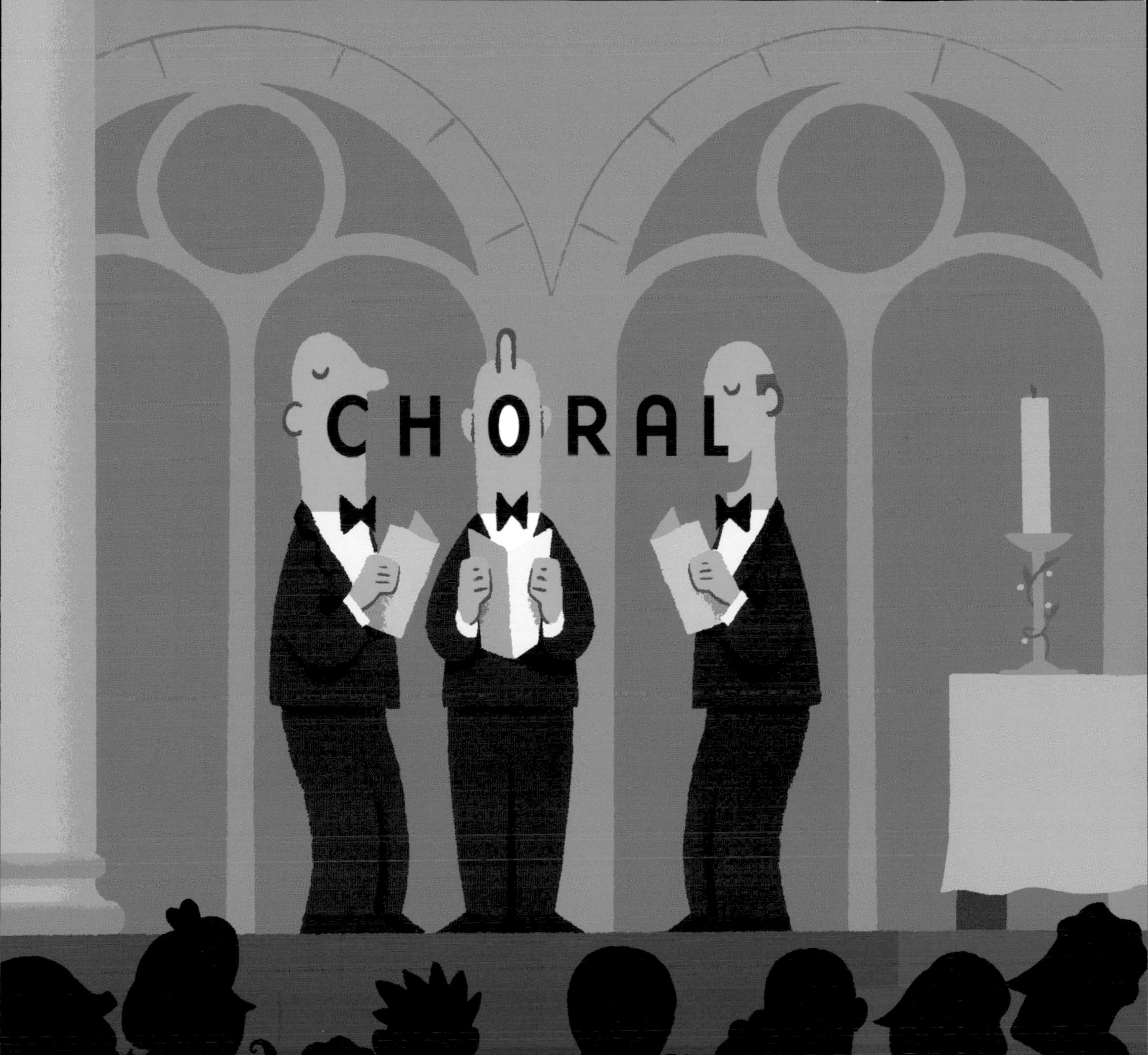
CHORAL

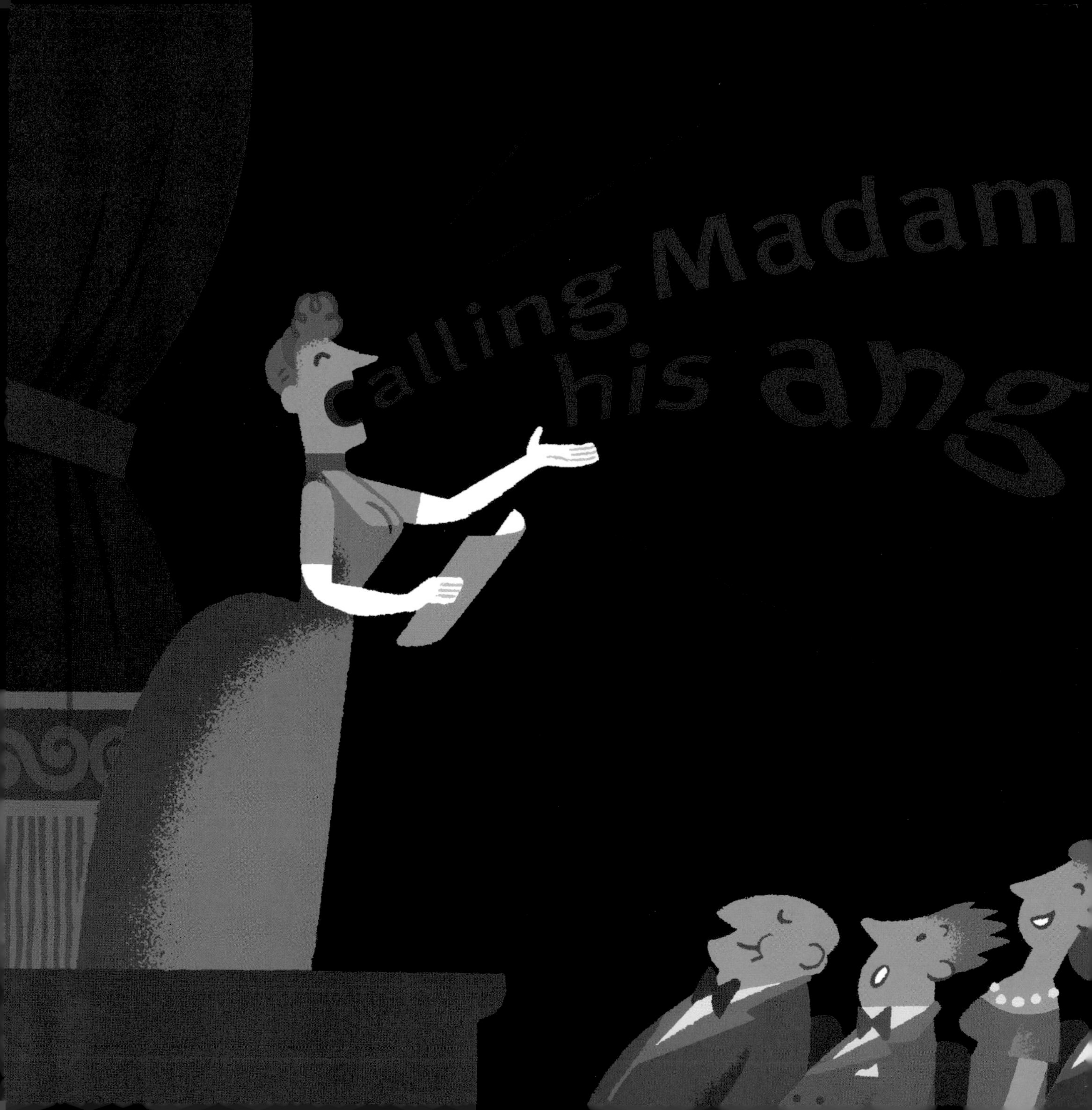
calling Madam
his ahng

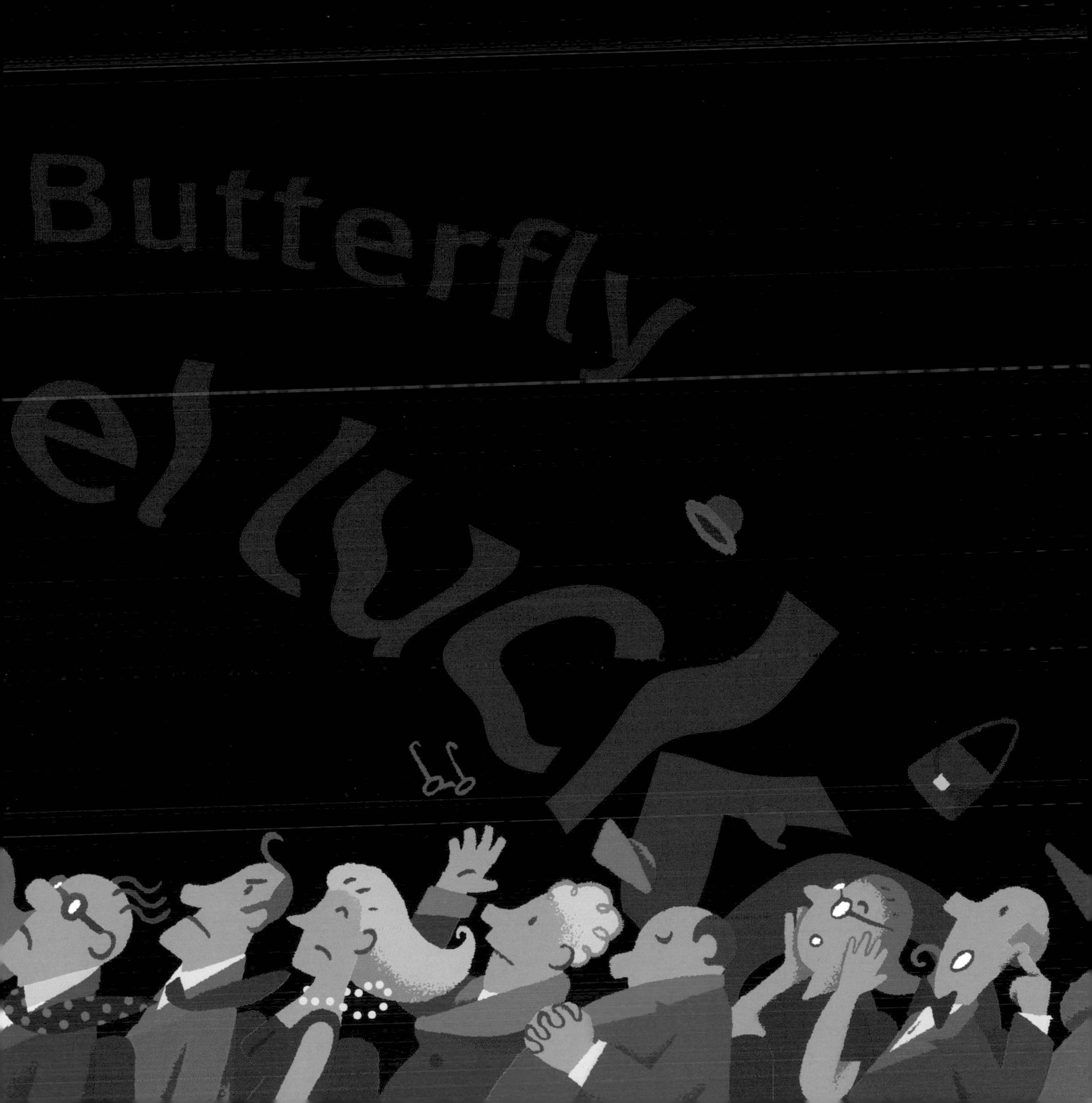
Butterfly

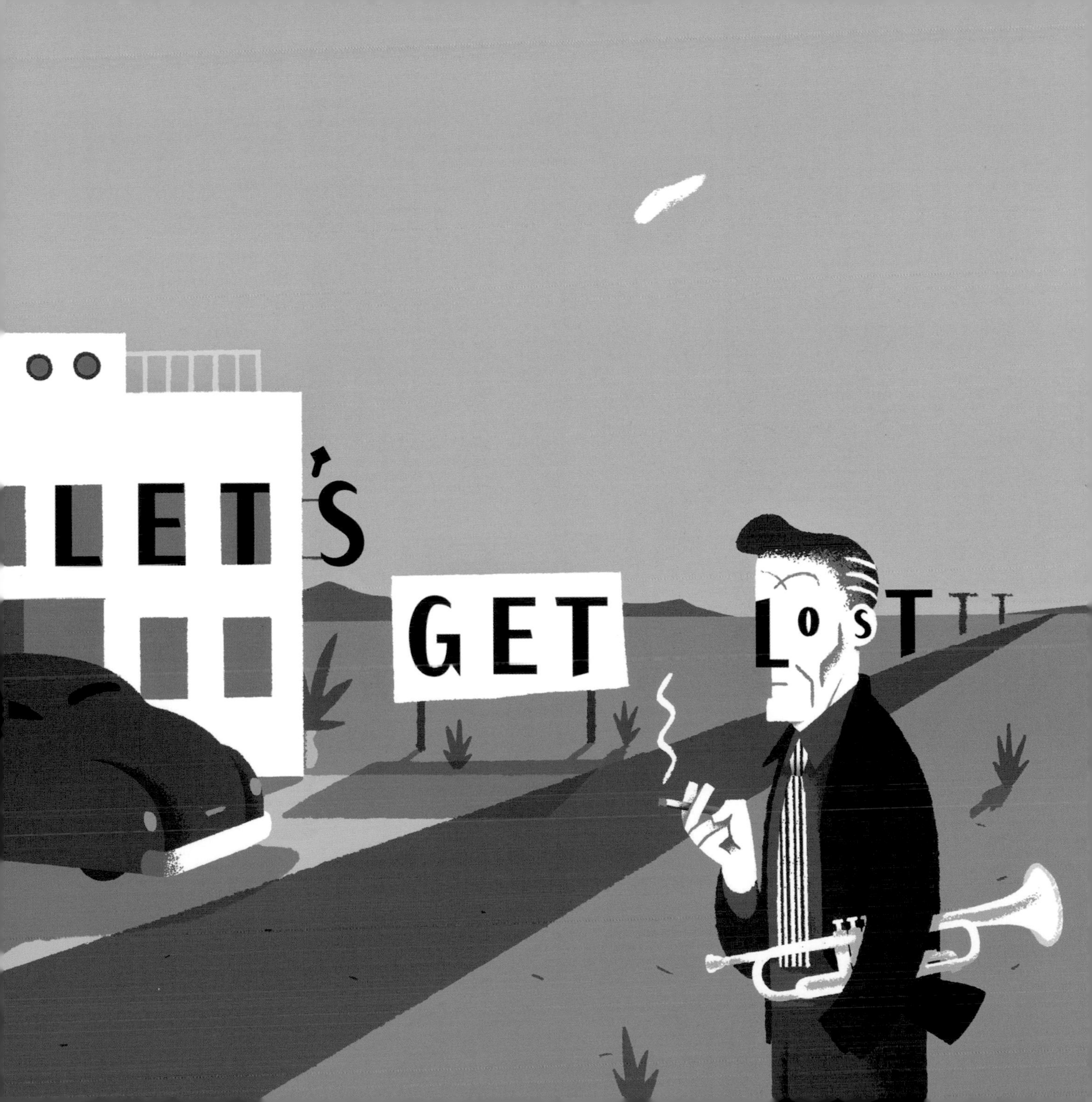
LET'S
GET
LOST